FOOTBALL FEVER!

Written
ALAN DURANT

Illustrated by
KATE LEAKE

MACMILLAN CHILDREN'S BOOKS

My little brother used to be normal.
He did the normal things that
little brothers do.

FOOTBALL FEVER!

For Kit,
with many happy memories ~ AD

For Rob & Chris ~ KL

First published 2006 by Macmillan Children's Books
This edition published 2006 by Macmillan Children's Books
a division of Macmillan Publishers Limited
20 New Wharf Road, London N1 9RR
Basingstoke and Oxford
Associated companies throughout the world
www.panmacmillan.com

ISBN: 978-1-4050-5566-6

A CIP catalogue record for this book is available from the British Library.

Printed in China

He dressed up as
a pirate.

He snuggled up on the sofa and watched cartoons.

He played games with me —

and lost.

Then he caught . . .

FEVER!

I think he caught it off Dad. Mum says
Dad's had football fever since he was a boy.
She says there's no cure.

My little brother doesn't
have spots or a rash.
He doesn't really look
any different.

But he acts CRAZY!

He can't stop kicking things.
He rolls up his socks and
kicks them up and down the hall.

He kicks stones along the pavement.

He kicks balls in the garden.

Sometimes he kicks me – but he doesn't mean to. That's just the way it is when you've got football fever.

All he talks about is football football football.

and . . .

"William, you're making my head spin," says Mum.

"He can't help it," I say. "He's got football fever."

Dad said, "I think it's time I took you to a club to play proper football."
"YES!" shouted my little brother. He punched the air and put his shirt over his head.

Last Sunday Dad took my little brother to a football club. I had to go too. "The fresh air will do you good," Dad said.

FOOTBALL
EVERY
SUNDAY

There were lots of children there — some my little brother's age, some a bit older, like me.

First they did some training.

They practised passing and shooting and kicking a ball between a line of cones.

My little brother wasn't very good at this. He knocked most of the cones over!

Then the children were put into teams to play a match.

My little brother was very excited. His team wore red shirts.

My little brother ran up and down like
a madman. He chased and he chased,
but he couldn't catch up with the ball.

But he was still
grinning like crazy.
"This is great!"
he yelled.

Then my
little brother
started to kick
the ball . . .

. . . but
not always
in the right
direction.

Once the ball hit
him in the face.
After that he stopped
running for a bit.

But then the fever came
back and he started
chasing the ball again.

At half-time
the score
was nil-nil.
No one had
scored a goal.

In the second half my little brother ran about more than ever. The ball went up one end, and then down the other — and my little brother went with it.

"COME

ON, WILLIAM!"

I shouted. I really wanted the Reds to win.

Suddenly one of the big boys in my little brother's team got the ball and ran up the field.

My little brother ran up the field behind him.
The big boy passed the ball to my little brother.

He was right in front of the goal.
"Shoot!" Dad shouted. I wanted to shout too,
but I was too excited.
My little brother kicked the ball . . .

. . . and fell over.

But the ball rolled in.

"GOAL!"

Dad and I jumped up and down and
hugged each other.
My little brother ran around the pitch
waving his hands in the air.

It was his first goal — and it
was the winner. The Reds had
won the match!

Now my little brother's got football fever worse than ever.

But guess what?

Next Sunday I'm
going to play at
the club with him . . .

... because I've got FOOTBALL FEVER too!